This book belongs to:

G
....

....

....

Retold by Gaby Goldsack
Illustrated by Ruth Galloway (Advocate)
Designed by Jester Designs

Language consultant: Betty Root

ISBN 1-84461-214-7

Marks and Spencer p.l.c.
PO Box 3339, Chester CH99 9QS
www.marksandspencer.com

MARKS &
SPENCER

The
Ugly Duckling

Helping your Child to Read

Learning to read is an exciting challenge for most children. From a very early age, sharing story books with children, talking about the pictures and guessing what might happen next are all very important parts of the reading experience.

Sharing reading

Set aside a regular quiet time to share reading with younger children, or to be on hand to encourage older children as they develop into independent readers.

First Readers are intended to encourage and support the early stages of learning to read. They present well-loved tales that children will happily listen to again and again. Familiarity helps children to identify some of the words and phrases.

When you feel your child is ready to move on a little, encourage him or her to join in so that you read the story aloud together. Always pause to talk about the pictures. The easy-to-read speech bubbles in **First Readers** provide an excellent 'joining-in' activity. The bright, clear illustrations and matching text will help children to understand the story.

Building confidence

In time, children will want to read *to* you. When this happens, be patient and give continual praise. They may not read all the words correctly, but children's substitutions are often very good guesses.

The repetition in each book is particularly helpful for building confidence. If your child cannot read a particular word, go back to the beginning of the sentence and read it together so the meaning is not lost. Most importantly, do not continue if your child is tired or simply in need of a change.

Reading alone

The next step is for your child to read alone. Try to be on hand to give help and support. Remember to give lots of encouragement and praise.

Together with other simple stories, **First Readers** will ensure that children will find reading an enjoyable and rewarding experience.

One day a mother duck sat on her nest.
She was waiting for her eggs to hatch.

She waited and waited.

Then, crack! They started to hatch.

crack!

9

Out popped three fluffy yellow
ducklings.

Now there was just one egg left. It was
a very big egg. The mother duck sat
back down.

Come on, hatch!

She waited and waited. She thought it would never hatch.

Then, crack! It started to hatch.

Out popped a big grey duckling.

The grey duckling looked big and ugly.

The mother duck took her new ducklings down to the pond. She showed them how to swim.

Soon they could all swim.

Even the big grey duckling.

The mother duck was
very pleased.

The mother duck took her new ducklings up to the farm.

All the animals thought the grey duckling was ugly.

"What an ugly duckling!" they said.

So the ugly duckling ran away.

He ran to the other side of the pond.
Wild ducks lived on the other side of
the pond.

The wild ducks thought the grey
duckling was ugly.

"What an ugly duckling!" they said.

So the ugly duckling ran away.

He ran to a cottage. An old woman
lived in the cottage. She lived with a cat
and a hen.

The cat and the hen thought the big duckling was ugly.

"What an ugly duckling!" they said.

So the ugly duckling ran away.

He ran to the lake.

One day he saw some swans fly by.

They were beautiful.

"I wish I looked like that,"
said the ugly duckling.

Winter came. It grew colder and colder.

The lake turned to ice.

The ugly duckling got stuck in the ice.

A farmer found him.

He took him home.

The farmer's children wanted to play with the ugly duckling. The ugly duckling was frightened.
So the duckling ran away.

He ran back to the pond.
He stayed there until spring.

The sun came out. The ugly duckling
flapped his wings. They felt strong.

He flapped and flapped until he was
flying high in the air.

The ugly duckling flew back to the lake.

He saw three beautiful swans on the lake

The ugly duckling landed on the lake. He looked at himself in the lake.

He was not an ugly duckling.
He was a beautiful swan.

I'm not ugly!

"Be our friend!" said the other swans.

The ugly duckling had some friends
at last.

Read and Say

How many of these words can you say?
The pictures will help you. Look back in
your book and see if you can find the
words in the story.

hen

cat

cottage

duck

ducklings

eggs

farmer

farm

pond

swans

Titles in this series, subject to availability:

Beauty and the Beast
Chicken-Licken
Cinderella
The Elves and the Shoemaker
The Emperor's New Clothes
The Enormous Turnip
The Gingerbread Man
Goldilocks and the Three Bears
Hansel and Gretel
Jack and the Beanstalk
Joseph's Coat of Many Colours
and Other Bible Stories
Little Red Riding Hood
Noah's Ark and Other Bible Stories
Rapunzel
Rumpelstiltskin
Sleeping Beauty
Snow White and the Seven Dwarfs
The Three Billy Goats Gruff
The Three Little Pigs
The Ugly Duckling